Garth Williams's
FURRY TALES

A GOLDEN BOOK • NEW YORK

CONTENTS

All titles illustrated by Garth Williams

ANIMAL FRIENDS

By Jane Werner Watson • Illustrated by Garth Williams

Once upon a time, in a small house deep in the woods, lived a lively family of animals.

There were Miss Kitty and Mr. Pup,
Brown Bunny, Little Chick, Fluffy Squirrel,
Poky Turtle, and Tweeter Bird.

Each had his little chest and his little bed and chair, and they took turns cooking on their little kitchen stove.

They got along nicely when it came to sharing toys, being quiet at nap times, and keeping the house neat. But they could not agree on food.

When Miss Kitty cooked, they had milk and catnip tea and little bits of liver on their plates.

Pup didn't mind the liver, but the rest were unhappy.

And they didn't like any better the juicy bones
Pup served them in his turn.

When Bunny fixed the meals, she arranged lettuce
leaves and carrot nibbles with artistic taste, but only
Tweeter Bird would eat any of them. And when
Tweeter served worms, and crispy, chewy seeds, only
Little Chick would eat them.

Little Chick liked bugs and beetles even better. Poky Turtle would nibble at them, but what he really hungered for were tasty ants' eggs. Fluffy Squirrel wanted nuts and nuts and nuts. Without his sharp teeth and his firm paws, the others could not get a nibble from a nut, so they all went hungry when Fluffy got the meals.

Finally they all knew something must be done.
They gathered around the fire one cool and cozy
evening and talked things over.

"The home for me," said Mr. Pup, wistfully, "is a place where I can have lots of bones and meat every day."

"I want milk and liver instead of bugs and seeds," said Miss Kitty, daintily smoothing her skirt. "That's the kind of home for me."

"Nuts for me," said Squirrel. "And I'll get them myself."

"Ants' eggs," yawned Turtle.

"Crispy lettuce," whispered Bunny.

"A stalk of seeds," dreamed Bird, "and some worms make a home for me."

"New homes are what we need," said Mr. Pup. And everyone agreed.

So bright and early next morning they packed their little satchels and they said their fond good-byes.

Squirrel did not pack. He waved good-bye to them all. For he had decided to stay in the house in the woods.

He started right in to gather nuts.

Soon there were nuts in the kitchen stove, nuts in the cupboards, nuts piled up in all the empty beds. There was scarcely room for that happy little Squirrel.

15

The others hopped along till they came to a
garden with rows and rows of tasty growing things.

"Here's the home for me," said bright-eyed
Brown Bunny, and she settled down there at the
roots of a big tree.

Little Chick found a chicken yard full of lovely scratchy gravel where lived all kinds of crispy, crunchy bugs.

"Here I stay," chirped Chick, squeezing under the fence to join the other chickens there.

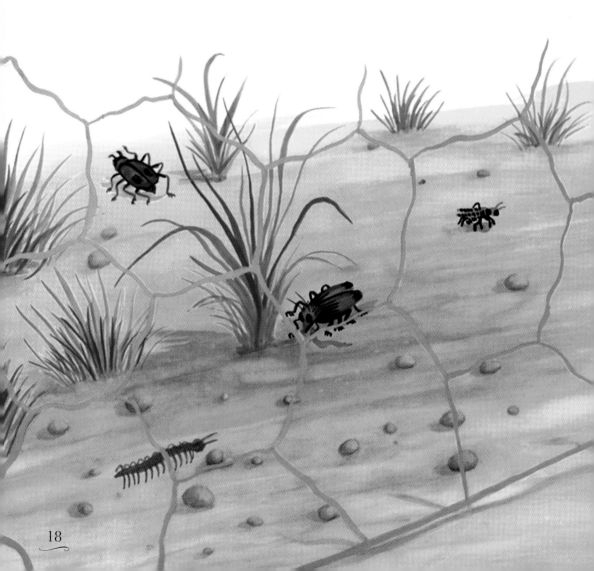

19

Poky Turtle found a pond with a lovely log for napping, half in the sun, half in the shade.

Close by the log was a busy, bustling ant hill, full of the eggs Turtle loved.

Tweeter Bird found a nest in a tree above the pond, where he could see the world, the seeds on the grasses, and the worms on the ground.

"This is the home for me," sang Bird happily.

Miss Kitty went on till she came to a house where a little girl welcomed her.

"Here is a bowl of milk for you, Miss Kitty," said the little girl, "and a ball of yarn to play with."

So Miss Kitty settled down in her new home with a purr.

Mr. Pup found a boy in the house next door.

The boy had a bone and some meat for Pup, a bed for him to sleep in, and a handsome collar to wear.

"Bow-wow," barked Pup. "This is the home for me."

That night each one said, as he went to sleep, "At last I've found the best home of all, the very best home for me."

Baby Animals

By Garth Williams

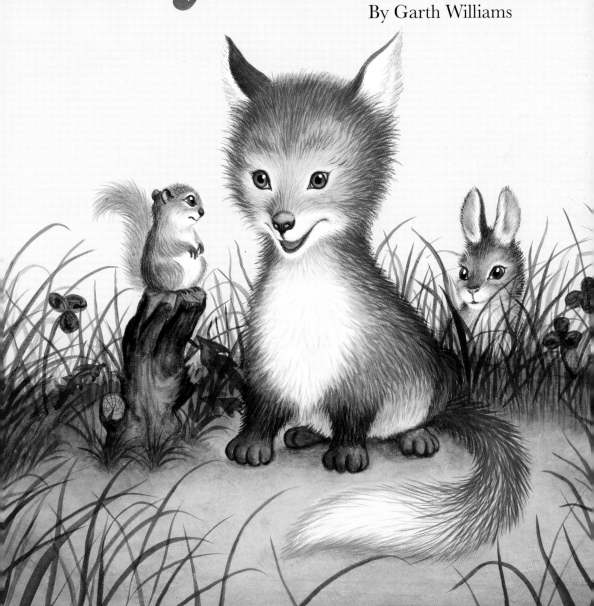

Baby Bear holds his toes. He wants to be
a circus bear when he grows up. He wants
to make all the children laugh.

Baby Squirrel has come to see what his
little cousin the chipmunk is so busy doing
at the end of the long branch.

Baby Chipmunk has a delicious nut and he is going to stuff it into his cheek before the baby squirrel gets it. They both like nuts to eat.

Baby Fox is full of mischief. He is hoping he will find a sleepy rabbit to chase, but the rabbits are hiding.

Baby Lamb is dancing over the hills
and meadows. It is spring and everyone
wants to dance after the cold winter.

Baby Opossum is pretending to be dead.
If a big bad dog comes along he will play
dead and the dog will go away.

Baby Skunk is fooled by his playmate
lying so still.

Baby Lion roars "Ahrrroum" just like
his father. One day he hopes he will be
king of the jungle.

Baby Tiger says, "You frighten me."
Baby Tiger looks like a great big kitten,
and he loves to play like one.

Baby Giraffe is so tall that he has to bend down to stay in the picture. He never makes a sound, and he can run very fast.

Baby Monkey swings from branch to
branch. He holds on with his two hands,
with his two feet, and with his tail.

Baby Orang-utan also lives in the trees. He is putting a leaf on his head to keep the sun off.

Baby Kangaroo hops like six rabbits.
He uses his big tail to keep his balance,
so he won't fall.

Baby Koala Bear lives in Australia
like Baby Kangaroo. He sleeps in the
eucalyptus tree at night and eats its
leaves in the daytime.

Baby Woodchuck has been asleep
all winter long. Now he is eating tender
grass and a small, tasty root. Soon he
will be very plump.

Baby Mink has just caught his first fish.
He is going to show it to his mother and
then eat it for breakfast.

Baby Rabbit has hopped away from his
mother's side. His eyes are wide open. He
sees a big bumblebee. "I don't think I will
go any farther," he says.

Baby Racoon washes his apple. He
never eats anything until he has washed
it first. He even washes a fish.

Baby Camel walks very well and can go for a day without drinking. He keeps food and water in his fat humps.

Baby Owl says, "Whooooooo's undressed
and whoooooo's in bed? Whooooooo's awake
and whooooooo's asleep?"

THE KITTEN
who thought he was a
MOUSE

By Miriam Norton
Illustrated by Garth Williams

There were five Miggses: Mother and
Father Miggs and Lester and two sisters.

They had, as field mice usually do, an outdoor
nest for summer in an empty lot and an indoor nest
for winter in a nearby house.

They were very surprised one summer day to find a strange bundle in their nest, a small gray and black bundle of fur and ears and legs, with eyes not yet open. They knew by its mewing that the bundle must be a kitten, a lost kitten with no family and no name.

"Poor kitty," said the sisters.

"Let him stay with us," said Lester.

"But a *cat*!" said Mother Miggs.

"Why not?" said Father Miggs.

"We can bring him up to be a good mouse. He
need never find out he is really a cat. You'll see—
he'll be a good thing for this family."

"Let's call him Mickey," said Lester.

And that's how Mickey Miggs found his new
family and a name.

After his eyes opened he began to grow up just
as mice do, eating all kinds of seeds and bugs and
drinking from puddles and sleeping in a cozy pile
of brother and sister mice.

Father Miggs showed him his first tomcat—at a
safe distance—and warned him to "keep away from
all cats and dogs and people."

Mickey saw his first mousetrap—"The most dangerous thing of all," said Mother Miggs— when they moved to the indoor nest that fall.

Mickey became useful in fooling the household cat, Hazel. He would hide in a dark corner and then, "Meow! Meow!" he'd cry. Hazel would poke around, leaving the pantry shelves unguarded while she looked for the other cat. That gave Lester and his sisters a chance to make a raid on the leftovers.

Poor Hazel! She knew she heard, even smelled, another cat, and sometimes saw a cat's eyes shining in a corner. But no cat ever came out to meet her.

How could she know that Mickey didn't know he was a cat at all and that he feared Hazel as much as the mousiest mouse would!

And so Mickey Miggs grew, becoming a better mouse all the time and enjoying his life. He loved cheese, bacon, and cake crumbs. He got especially good at smelling out potato skins and led the sisters and Lester straight to them every time.

"A wholesome and uncatlike food," said
Mother Miggs to Father Miggs approvingly.
"Mickey is doing well." And Father Miggs
said to Mother Miggs, "I told you so!"

Then one day, coming from a nap in the wastepaper basket, Mickey met the children of the house, Peggy and Paul.

"Ee-eeeeeek!" Mickey squeaked in terror. He dashed along the walls of the room looking for his mousehole.

"It's a kitten!" cried Peggy, as Mickey squeezed through the hole.

"But it acts like a mouse," said Paul.

The children could not understand why the kitten had been so mouselike, but they decided to try to make friends with him.

That night, as Mickey came out of his hole, he nearly tripped over something lying right there in front of him. He sniffed at it. It was a dish, and in the dish was something to drink.

"What is it?" asked Mickey. Lester didn't know, but timidly tried a little. "No good," he said, shaking his whiskers.

Mickey tried it, tried some more, then some more and some more and more and more—until it was all gone.

"*Mmmmmmmmmmm!*" he said. "What wonderful stuff."

"It's probably poison and you'll get sick," said Lester disgustedly. But it wasn't poison, and Mickey had a lovely feeling in his stomach from drinking it. It was milk, of course. And every night that week Mickey found a saucer of milk outside that same hole. He lapped up every drop.

"He drank it, he drank it!" cried Peggy and Paul happily each morning. They began to set out a saucerful in the daytime, too.

At first Mickey would drink the milk only when he was sure Peggy and Paul were nowhere around. Soon he grew bolder and began to trust them in the room with him.

And soon he began to let them come nearer and nearer and nearer still.

Then one day he found himself scooped up and held in Peggy's arms. He didn't feel scared. He felt fine. And he felt a queer noise rumble up his back and all through him. It was Mickey's first purr.

Peggy and Paul took Mickey to a shiny glass on the wall and held him close in front of it. Mickey, who had never seen a mirror, saw a cat staring at him there, a cat in Paul's arms where he thought *he* was. He began to cry, and his cry, instead of being a squeak, was a mewing wail.

Finally Mickey began to understand that he was not a mouse like Lester and his sisters, but a cat like Hazel.

He stayed with Peggy and Paul that night, trying not to be afraid of his own cat-self. He still didn't quite believe it all, however, and next morning he crept back through his old hole straight to Mother Miggs.

"Am I really a cat?" he cried.

"Yes," said Mother Miggs sadly. And she
told him the whole story of how he was adopted
and brought up as a mouse. "We loved you and
wanted you to love us," she explained. "It was
the only safe and fair way to bring you up."

After talking with Mother Miggs, Mickey decided to be a cat in all ways. He now lives with Peggy and Paul, who also love him, and who can give him lots of good milk and who aren't afraid of his purr or his meow.

Mickey can't really forget his upbringing, however. He takes an old rubber mouse of Peggy's to bed with him.

He often visits the Miggses in the indoor nest, where he nibbles cheese tidbits and squeaks about old times.

And of course he sees to it that Hazel no longer prowls in the pantry at night.

"Oh, I'm so fat and stuffed from eating so much in Hazel's pantry," Father Miggs often says happily to Mother Miggs. "I always said our Mickey would be a good thing for the family—and he is!"

Bunnies'
A B C

By Garth Williams

Aa

for alligator

Bb

for bear

Cc

for cat

Dd

for deer

Ee

for ermine

Ff

for fish

Gg

for giraffe

for horse

Ii

for ibis

Jj

for jaguar

Kk

for kangaroo

Ll

for ladybug

Mm

for mouse

Nn

for nightingale

Oo

for ostrich

Pp

for panda

Qq

for quail

Rr

for rooster

Ss

for seal

Tt

for turtle

Uu

for unicorn

Vv

for vulture

Ww

for walrus

Xx

for xenurus

Yy

for yak

Zz

THE
END

for zebra

THE
SAILOR DOG

By Margaret Wise Brown
Illustrated by Garth Williams

Born at sea in the teeth of a gale, the
sailor was a dog. Scuppers was his name.

After that he lived on a farm. But Scuppers,
born at sea, was a sailor. And when he grew
up, he wanted to go to sea.

So he went to look for something to go in.
He found a little submarine. "All aboard!"
they called. It was going down under the sea.
But Scuppers did not want to go under the sea.

He found a little car.

"All aboard!" they called. It was going over the land. But Scuppers did not want to go over the land.

Scuppers was a sailor. He wanted to go to sea.

So Scuppers went over the hills and far away until he came to the sea.

Over the hills and far away was the ocean. And on the ocean was a ship. The ship was about to go over the sea. It blew all its whistles.

"All aboard!" they called.

"All ashore that are going ashore!"

"All aboard!"

So Scuppers went to sea.

The ship began to move slowly along. The wind blew it.

In his ship Scuppers had a little room. In his room Scuppers had a hook for his hat and a hook for his rope and a hook for his handkerchief and a hook for his pants and a hook for his spyglass and a place for his shoes and a bunk for a bed to put himself in.

At night Scuppers threw the anchor into the
sea, and he went down to his little room.

He put his hat on the hook for his hat, and his rope on the hook for his rope, and his pants on the hook for his pants, and his spyglass on the hook for his spyglass, and he put his shoes under the bed and got into his bed, which was a bunk, and went to sleep.

Next morning he was shipwrecked.

Too big a storm blew out of the sky. The anchor dragged, and the ship crashed onto the rocks. There was a big hole in it.

Scuppers himself was washed overboard and hurled by huge waves onto the shore.

He was washed up onto the beach. It was foggy and rainy. There were no houses, and Scuppers needed a house.

But on the beach was lots and lots of driftwood, and he found an old rusty box stuck in the sand.

Maybe it was a treasure!

It was a treasure—to Scuppers.

It was an old-fashioned tool box with hammers and nails and an ax and a saw. Everything he needed to build himself a house. So Scuppers started to build a house, all by himself, out of driftwood.

He built a door and a window and a roof and a porch and a floor, all out of driftwood.

And he found some red bricks and built a big red chimney. And then he lit a fire, and the smoke went up the chimney.

Then the stars came out, and he was sleepy.
So he built a bed of pine branches.

And he jumped into his deep green bed and
went to sleep. As he slept he dreamed—

If he could build a house,
he could mend the hole in the ship.

So the next day at low tide he took his tool box and waded out and hammered planks across the hole in his ship.

At last the ship was fixed.

So he sailed away.

Until he came to a seaport in a foreign land.

By now his clothes were all worn and ripped and torn and blown to pieces. His coat was torn, his hat was blown away, and his shoes were all worn out. And his handkerchief was ripped. Only his pants were still good.

So he went ashore to buy some clothes at the Army and Navy Store. And some fresh oranges. He bought a coat. He found a red one too small. He found a blue one just right. It had brass buttons on it.

Then he went to buy a hat. He found a purple one too silly. He found a white one just right.

He needed new shoes. He found some yellow ones too small. He found some red ones too fancy. Then he found some white ones just right.

Here he is with his new hat on, and with his new shoes on, and with his new coat on, with his shiny brass buttons. (He has a can of polish and a cloth to keep them shiny.)

And he has a new clean handkerchief, and a new rope, and a bushel of oranges.

And now Scuppers wants to go back to his ship. So he goes there.

And at night when the stars came out, he took
one last look through his spyglass. And went down
below to his little room, and he hung his new hat
on the hook for his hat, and he hung his spyglass on
the hook for his spyglass, and he hung his new coat
on the hook for his coat, and his new handkerchief
on the hook for his handkerchief, and his pants on
the hook for his pants, and his new rope on the
hook for his rope, and his new shoes he put under
his bunk, and himself he put in his bunk.

And here he is where he wants to be—
a sailor sailing the deep green sea.

HIS SONG

I am Scuppers the Sailor Dog—
I'm Scuppers the Sailor Dog—
I can sail in a gale
right over a whale
under full sail
in a fog.

I am Scuppers the Sailor Dog—
I'm Scuppers the Sailor Dog—
with a shake and a snort
I can sail into port
under full sail
in a fog.

HOME FOR A BUNNY

By Margaret Wise Brown • Illustrated by Garth Williams

"Spring, Spring, Spring!"
sang the frog.
"Spring!"
said the groundhog.

"Spring, Spring, Spring!"
sang the robin.
It was Spring.
The leaves burst out.
The flowers burst out.
And robins burst out of their eggs.
It was Spring.

In the Spring a bunny
came down the road.
　He was going to find
a home of his own.
　A home for a bunny,
　A home of his own,
　Under a rock,
　Under a stone,
　Under a log,
　Or under the ground.
　Where would a bunny find a home?

"Where is your home?"
he asked the robin.

"Here, here, here,"
sang the robin.
"Here in this nest is my home."

"Here, here, here,"
sang the little robins who were
about to fall out of the nest.
"Here is our home."

"Not for me," said the bunny.
"I would fall out of a nest.
I would fall on the ground."

So he went on
looking for a home.
"Where is your home?"
he asked the frog.

"Wog, wog, wog,"
sang the frog.
"Wog, wog, wog,
Under the water,
Down in the bog."
    "Not for me,"
said the bunny.
"Under the water,
I would drown in a bog."

131

So he went on
looking for a home.
    "Where do you live?"
he asked the groundhog.
"In a log," said the groundhog.
"Can I come in?" said the bunny.
"No, you can't come in my log,"
    said the groundhog.

133

So the bunny went down the road.
Down the road
and down the road he went.
He was going to find
a home of his own.
A home for a bunny,
A home of his own,
Under a rock
Or a log
Or a stone.
Where would a bunny find a home?

Down the road
and down the road
and down the road
he went, until—

He met a bunny.
"Where is your home?"
he asked the bunny.

"Here," said the bunny.
"Here is my home.
Under this rock,
Under this stone,
Down under the ground,
Here is my home."

"Can I come in?"
said the bunny.
"Yes," said the bunny.
And so he did.

And that was his home.

A Tale of Tails

By Elizabeth H. MacPherson • Illustrated by Garth Williams

My dog has a tail he can wag when he's glad.

My cat has a tail she can swish when she's mad.

A very fine tail has the big kangaroo,

And so has the lion that lives in the zoo.

The horse has a tail for brushing off flies.

An elephant's tail is quite small for his size.

A monkey can swing by his tail from a tree.

Oh, everyone has a tail except me.

A fish has a tail that can help him to swim.

A mouse has a tail that is longer than him.

The tail of the rabbit is fluffy and small.

The tail of the whale is the largest of all.

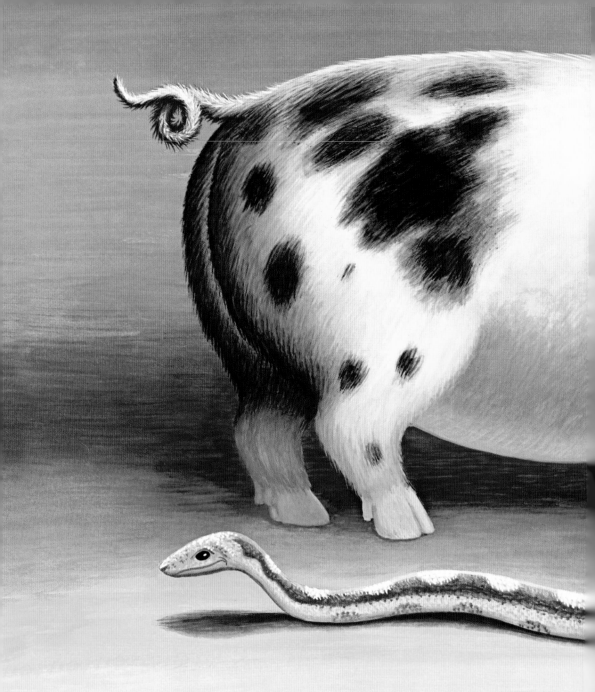

The pig has a tail with a curl and a bend.

A snake is all tail with a head on one end.

A polliwog's tail disappears as he grows.
And even a snail has a tail, I suppose.

The little gray squirrels that live in our tree
Have tails that are bushy as bushy can be.

And such a small tail has the big polar bear
I doubt very much that he knows it is there.

A bird has a tail that can help him to fly.

If they all have tails, then why haven't I?

The Friendly Book

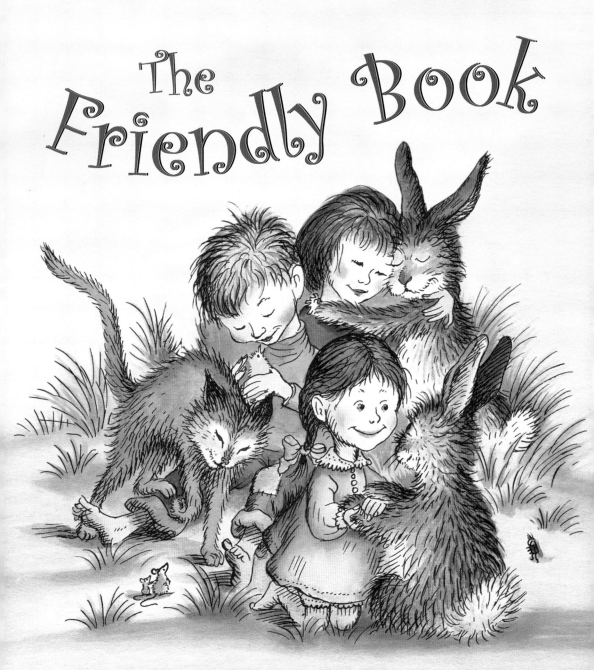

By Margaret Wise Brown • Illustrated by Garth Williams

I LIKE CARS

Red cars   Green cars

Sport limousine cars

I like cars
A car in a garage
A car with a load
A car with a flat tire
A car on the road
I like cars.

I LIKE TRAINS

Express trains
Toy trains
Streamline trains
Freight trains
Old trains
Milk trains

Any kind of train
A train in the station
Trains crossing the plains

Trains in a snowstorm
Trains in the rain
I like trains.

I LIKE STARS

Yellow stars
Green stars
Red stars
Blue stars
I like stars
Far stars
Quiet stars
Bright stars
Light stars
I like stars

A star that is shooting across the dark sky
A star that is shining right straight in your eye
I like stars.

I LIKE SNOW

Cold snow
Slow snow
White snow
Icy snow
I like snow
Snow falling softly with everything still
White in the blue night, white on the sill
White on the trees on the far distant hill
With everything still
I like snow.

I LIKE FISH

Silver fish   Gold fish
Black fish   Old fish
Young fish   Fishy fish
Any kind of fish

A fish in a pond
A fish in a stream
A fish in the ocean
A fish in a dream
I like fish.

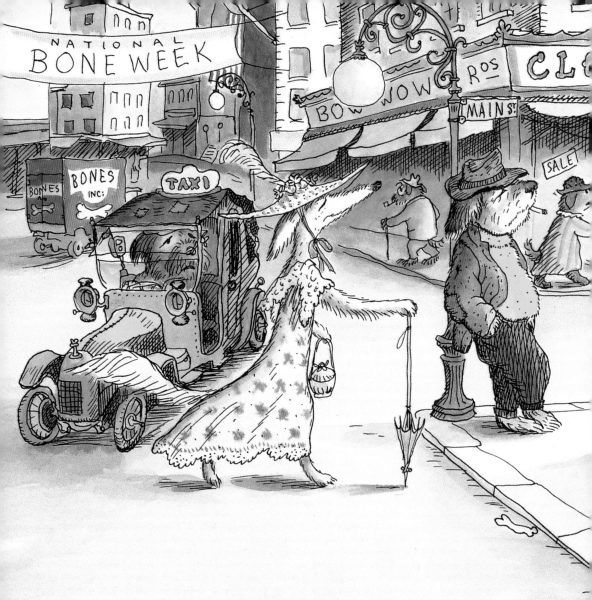

I LIKE DOGS

Big dogs   Little dogs
Fat dogs   Doggy dogs
Old dogs   Puppy dogs

183

I like dogs
A dog that is barking over the hill
A dog that is dreaming very still
A dog that is running wherever he will
I like dogs.

I LIKE BOATS

Any kind of boat

Tug boats   Tow boats

Large boats   Barge boats

Sail boats   Whale boats
Thin boats   Skin boats
Rubber boats   River boats
Flat boats   Cat boats
U boats   New boats

Tooting boats   Hooting boats
South American fruit boats
Bum boats   Gun boats
Slow boats   Row boats
I like boats.

I LIKE PEOPLE

Glad people
Sad people
Slow people
Mad people
Big people
Little people

I like people.

BABY FARM ANIMALS

By Garth Williams

Baby Sheep is called a lamb. He likes to run in the grass that grows in the meadow.

Baby Cats are called kittens. They love playing
on the farm. At night the farmer gives them cow's
milk, and they curl up together in the big red barn.

Baby Rabbit lives in a hutch, which is her
tiny little house. She sniffs noses with the kittens
and puppies because they are all friends.

Baby Guinea Pigs also have a hutch.
Have you ever seen a guinea pig's tail?

"That rabbit has been up to some
mischief," says the brown guinea pig.

Baby Donkey loves to eat juicy
carrots. He is sitting down because he
is tired. Somebody is trying to make
him stand up and follow those carrots
tied on the end of a stick.

"I know that trick," he says.

199

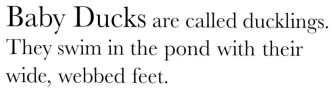

Baby Ducks are called ducklings. They swim in the pond with their wide, webbed feet.

"Why don't you come for a swim?" they ask the little chicks.

Baby Chickens are called
chicks. They cannot swim.

"Mother says we must look for
worms and stay out of the water,"
they reply.

Baby Pigs are called piglets. They love clean straw to sleep on. A piglet digs with his nose, which is called a snout. If you pick him up or chase him, he will squeal for his mother: "Help, help, help!"

Baby Dogs are called puppies. They stay in the stable, close to the horses. They growl and bark at strangers. They pretend that the shoe is a big cat. They growl and bark at it, too.

Baby Goats are called kids, just
as little boys and girls are. They try
to knock each other down by butting
their heads together. Their father has
horns and a pointed beard.

Baby Swans are called cygnets. Now they are covered with smoke-colored down, but soon they will have pure white feathers and long, long necks.

Baby Goose is called a gosling. She will be a big gray goose someday. See her brother with his head under the water. He is looking for something to eat.

Baby Horse we call a foal. She could walk the same day she was born. Now, after a week, she gallops. When she is two years old, she will be a beautiful horse, and she will be able to carry a rider on her back. Perhaps she will even win a race.

Baby Pony is taking Kitten and Puppy for a ride. He is a Shetland pony, so he will not grow very much bigger.

Baby Cow is called a calf. She says, "Moooo!
It is time for lunch."